MW00983362

Three

For my brother Dave

Special thanks to Margaret Connolly, Ana Vivas, Andrew Berkhut, Tiffany Malins, Trish, Tanith, and Luka.

Neal Porter Books

First published by Scholastic Australia in 2019.
Text and illustrations copyright © Stephen Michael King, 2019
All rights reserved.
First published in the United States of America in 2021 by
Holiday House Publishing, Inc., New York
Printed and bound in December 2020 at Leo Paper, Heshan, China.
The artwork for this book was created using graphite pencil, watercolor, felt-tip pen, and ink.
www.holidayhouse.com
First Edition
1   3   5   7   9   10   8   6   4   2

Library of Congress Cataloging-in-Publication Data

Names: King, Stephen Michael, author.
Title: Three / by Stephen Michael King.
Other titles: 3
Description: First American edition. | New York : Holiday House / Neal
Porter Books, 2021. | "First published by Scholastic Australia in 2019."
| Audience: Ages 4 to 8. | Audience: Grades K–1. | Summary: Three, a
homeless three-legged dog, skips and hops about the city until he
befriends a little girl who accepts him as he is.
Identifiers: LCCN 2020011211 | ISBN 9780823449231 (hardcover)
Subjects: CYAC: Dogs—Fiction. | Acceptance—Fiction. | Gratitude—Fiction.
Classification: LCC PZ7.K58915 Th 2021 | DDC [E]—dc23
LC record available at https://lccn.loc.gov/2020011211

ISBN 978-0-8234-4923-1 (hardcover)

Three

Stephen Michael King

NEAL PORTER BOOKS

HOLIDAY HOUSE/NEW YORK

One . . .

two . . .

three.

One . . .

two . . .

three.

Every day was a skip

and a hop

for Three.

When the sun was shining,
he was warm.

If it rained all day,
he felt clean . . .

and his waggly tail
    kept him well fed.

Occasionally,
he looked
for a home,

or

for

someone

to

love,

but

mostly

he

walked
from   here

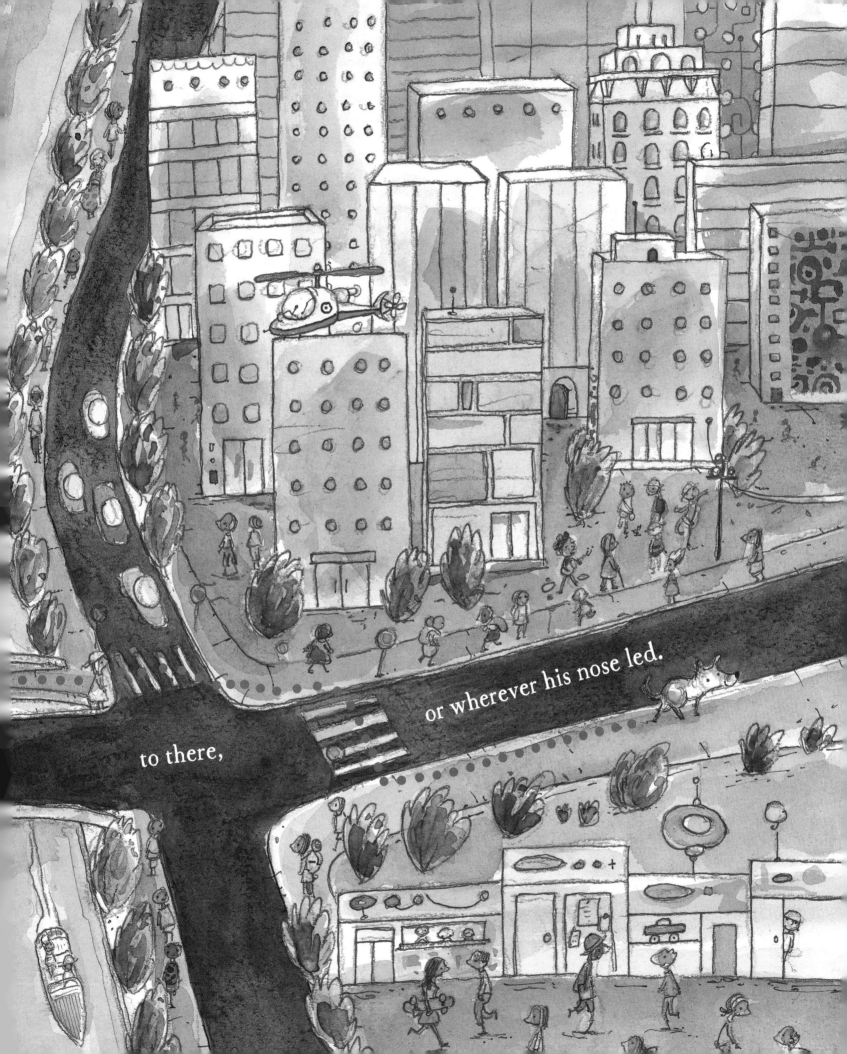

to there,

or wherever his nose led.

Three sniffed his way
and found a six leg.

Living in the city was hard
for little six legs.

Three was happy that little six legs
had an underground home, far away
from busy feet.

Three sniffed his way
and found an eight leg.

Living in the city was hard
for little eight legs too.

Three was happy that the little eight leg
had a home up high, far away
from busy traffic.

Three was thankful that he
didn't have more legs than he
could count . . .

or longer legs than he needed.

He was happy he didn't have four legs.

If Three had four legs, he might be a chair.
Chairs didn't go anywhere, and the
two legs sat all over them.

Three was thankful that his legs
took him wherever he chose,
and that he knew how to cross
a road when the light was green.

One day, Three followed a sweet-scented breeze

and found he had walked far away

to a place where the green rolled slowly,

and the cars were not so many.

Three met a four leg with two spikes on its head . . .

and a winged two leg that laid eggs.

He met a pink four leg that snorted
through its flat, friendly nose,

and a little something that had
two big ears and two big feet.

Three met a two leg pretending
to be a three leg, just like him.

She poured him a glass of milk and shared her cookies.

The girl talked with Three.
Her name was Fern.

Fern also talked to herself

and talked with the trees

and talked to the . . .

. . . garden.

Fern's garden was a happy home
for six legs and eight legs.

But there were also creatures
that Three had rarely seen before:
hopping four legs, flying six legs,
and sliding no legs.

Inside Fern's home they met
a one leg
and a
twelve leg.

Fern asked Three if he would stay forever, so that
Fern, her mother, her brother, and Three would make . . .

a perfect four.

Fern made Three his own special
curl-up place where he'd feel
warm and safe.

And on Saturdays they always had pancakes with ice cream for breakfast.

Fern was thankful

for her new friend . . .

. . . and Three was thankful
for Fern.